T0196074

The Community Club

#1 Aubrey and the Fight for LIfe

Shannon Simmons

iUniverse, Inc.

New York   Bloomington

iUniverse books may be ordered through booksellers or by contacting:

iUniverse
1663 Liberty Drive
Bloomington, IN 47403
www.iuniverse.com
1-800-Authors (1-800-288-4677)

Because of the dynamic nature of the Internet, any Web addresses or
links contained in this book may have changed since publication and
may no longer be valid. The views expressed in this work are solely those
of the author and do not necessarily reflect the views of the publisher,
and the publisher hereby disclaims any responsibility for them.

ISBN: 978-1-4401-7616-6 (sc)
ISBN: 978-1-4401-7617-3 (ebook)

Printed in the United States of America

iUniverse rev. date: 10/15/2009

Chapter One:

"Who knows what causes cancer?" Mrs. Wellborne asked. My hand shot up.

"Yes, little girl in pink?"

I opened my mouth, then frowned. I hate when people call me 'little girl'. I'm not little! Plus, if I know her name, she should know mine.

I'm Aubrey Addison. I'm eleven, and in fifth grade. A lot of my friends would say, "Above all, Aubrey is generous." I guess that's true, since I formed a club, the Community Club (or CC), that's about helping people, which I'll tell you about later. I'm also smart, kind, and way too outgoing for my own good.

One thing about me that you can't really tell just by looking at me is that I don't have a mom. I'm adopted, from Japan. My dad adopted me when I was a baby. People sometimes ask whether or not I wish I knew my real mom and dad, and I say no, because when I think about living with anybody else, or going to Japan and leaving New Jersey, I start to cry.

I've lived in that same house, 357 Buckwell Drive in Amesville, New Jersey all my life (well, except the month and a half in Japan, of course).

I guess you've already figured out that I have long, straight black hair and brown eyes, right? And you might know I'm looking forward to next year, when we go into World History (by the way, I love history), which means I'll be able to learn about Japan. I'm really excited.

Well, there's my life story. Back to that day. Mrs. Wellborne only comes once a month, during history (boo), to tell us about health. Today we were talking about cancer. It was already May, so kids were dreaming about summer vacation. Worse, (for her) it was Friday, so no one was paying much attention to her.

"Well, you can get lung, mouth, and throat cancer from smoking, and sometimes even by being around someone who smokes," I answered.

She nodded.

"Ow!" I turned around. Jason Park was playing with his plastic airplanes again. One had hit my back. I rolled my eyes as his best friend, Michael Baker, laughed at me. Boys are so immature.

I got a 'shh' sign from Mrs. Wellborne, which set everyone else off laughing. I wanted to scream at them, but I didn't. Instead I turned around in my chair. My friends looked at me sympathetically. I shrugged, then turned my attention back to the board. Two more airplanes hit, but I just let them fall to the floor, and eventually they stopped.

As soon as the lunch bell rang, I sped from my seat

to the door. My best friend, Jenna, was next in line. We walked silently through the lunch line, as the lunch ladies gave us our food, then we found an empty table to sit at. We started talking nonstop.

"That was so unfair. You got hit by something Ms. Mathews told Jason not to bring to school, and you're blamed. I think Mrs. Wellborne has to be the worst teacher I've ever had," Jenna said as she picked through her lunch. I shrugged. She kept going, but I started thinking. What if someone in the neighborhood had cancer? What if someone at school had cancer? How would we know if someone did? Would the teachers go on a search for why that person had cancer? Mm.

Then I made up a story to go with it. It was far-fetched, but I never care about that kind of stuff.

In it, it was the Monday after Mrs. Wellborne's next appearance. It was time for history, and Mrs. Wellborne came in. The class gasped.

"I have news that someone in here has cancer," she said.

I shrunk in my seat. She hated me. "Addison!" she shouted. "Sit up straight or go to . . . my lair (hey, I already admitted it was far-fetched)." The entire class gasped again. I sat up, and started crying. "No crying, Addison! Or it's the lair for you."

I dried my eyes. It turned out a girl named Mariah had cancer. Everyone started crying. No one got yelled at. I raised my hand. So did Jenna.

"What?" Mrs. Wellborne barked at us. We told her about our club. Just as we were being lifted onto our classmates' shoulders . . .

The bell rang in real life. I jerked up and realized I hadn't even touched my food. Oh, well. Too late now.

That afternoon I was supposed to go over to Jenna's to baby-sit. Her step dad was at work (more about all this later), her mom was about to take two of her big brothers somewhere, and her oldest brother was assigned the job of taking her to her softball practice, which cleared the house except her nine-year-old sister, Faith, so I agreed to take care of her. She's really not much of a problem, especially since she and Jenna are really friends (good thing, too, because they share a room). Anyway, Jenna would be back by five, so it was only an hour and a half long job. But, since school got out half an hour early that day (no one knows why), I had an hour to spend with my dad before I left for my baby-sitting job.

I usually walk home, but that day I'd brought my bike, since I thought I'd have to go straight to Jenna's, which takes longer than the walk to my house.

So when school got out, I hopped on my bike and headed home, preparing a mini speech for my dad, in case he thought something was wrong. When I got home, I left my bike latched to a pole, and ran inside.

"Dad?" I called, as I walked inside. I checked his office. He works at home, so he can spend the most possible time with me, I think in an effort to stop me from wishing my real parents lived with me. Anyway, he wasn't there. I found him sitting at the dining room table, working. When he saw me, he looked up, then down at his watch. "School was let out early," I explained.

"Oh. I was thinking you teleported." I laughed. My dad has a great sense of humor.

"So, what would you like to do for the next fifteen minutes, Aubs?" (only my dad calls me 'Aubs')

I thought for a minute. "I think I'll go upstairs and do a little bit of cleaning in my room."

He looked at me. "You okay?"

I giggled. "Yes. Jenna says she thinks there'll be another business trip coming up, so I want it clean for her."

He nodded. "Carry on, then. I was just looking for a change of scenery."

"Or a TV," I teased. Then I went upstairs, closed my bedroom door, and started picking up pieces of clothing and putting them in the closet. It seemed like one minute later when there was a knock on my door. "Come in," I said absent-mindedly.

Dad stuck his head in. "It's three twenty. Want me to drive you to Jenna's?"

Oh, no! "Yes." I raced downstairs and out to the garage, then climbed in Dad's car. He got in and drove me to Jenna's house. When we got there, I rang the doorbell. Jenna answered.

"Hi," she said.

I waved. "Sorry I was almost late."

"It's okay. Come on in. My mom already left, and we're about to leave. You know where the numbers are, and we'll just be at the field, so call my mom or my cell phone if something happens. Am I forgetting something? Oh, yeah. Faith. She's in the den, I think. She might have gone upstairs though."

Her brother stepped into the foyer at the same time I did. "Let's go, or you'll be late."

After her brother gave me some instructions about rules (most of which I knew), they left. I stepped into the den. No Faith. So I went upstairs, and into her room. I found her on her bed, staring into space. I looked around. She seemed to be staring at the desk, but I wasn't sure. I turned around to walk out of the room and go downstairs.

"No, don't!" I jumped a mile.

"Don't what? Leave? I was just going to go downstairs and get you a snack. Are you okay?"

Faith shook her head. "I'm far from okay. How many days of school are left?"

"Ten," I answered. "Why?"

She looked at me for the first time since I'd gotten there. "What's fourth grade like?" she asked.

I shrugged and sat down on Jenna's bed, so we could face each other. "It's basically the same as third grade, but you learn different stuff. And when you're in fourth grade, teachers usually don't just give out homework. They give you stuff to do that's due the next day, and if you don't finish in class, it's homework. Pretty simple system."

"This isn't funny. It's my first year at elementary school without Jenna."

"No, it's not," I said. "What about kindergarten and first grade? You know, before you guys knew each other?"

"Seth was in fifth grade when I was in first. Then Dad married Sara, and while Seth went to middle school, Jenna was in fourth grade. Now I'm in fourth grade and everyone else is in middle school or high school."

"So? What difference does it make?"

She sighed. "Aubrey, Aubrey, Aubrey. I'm going to be completely on my own!"

"Just because all your brothers and Jenna have graduated from elementary school doesn't mean you're alone."

"Yeah, it basically does."

"Faith, maybe it's your turn to be the big kid."

She looked up at me. "What do you mean?"

"Well, what about Logan and Brianna? You know, Erin's little brother and Brooke's little sister?"

"I know them. So?"

"So, they're in second and third grade, and their sisters are leaving elementary school, too. They need someone else to look up to. You can be that someone, can't you?"

"I guess. But I'm not Jenna. Jenna's perfect."

"Yeah, right! Jenna's far from perfect, just like everyone else in the universe. You're just as good as her. Besides, what has Jenna done for you over the years?"

Faith shrugged. "Nothing, really. She was just . . . there. You know?"

"I know. And I know you can be there for Brianna and Logan. Okay?"

"Okay. And Aubrey?"

"Yeah?"

"Can I have that snack now?"

I laughed. "Sure. I think it's still early enough that your brother wouldn't mind. It's four."

She nodded. "Okay. What did he say I could have?"

"He said he set out stuff for us to get a PB&J sandwich to share. Does that sound good?"

"Yeah!"

We walked downstairs together and found our ingredients on the kitchen table, right where I'd been told they were. I made a peanut butter and jelly sandwich and cut it into two triangles, giving one to Faith. As we were eating, the kitchen phone rang.

"Hello, Morris-Heller residence," I said.

"Hi, Aubrey. It's Brooke. I'm over at Erin's house, and Logan just broke something I think. It was an important vase, he says. But that's not why I'm calling. He needs stitches."

"What?!"

"Yeah, plus I have Brianna. Could you come over and bring Faith so I can make some phone calls?"

"No problem. We'll be right over. Let me leave a note, and we'll be there as fast as we can."

I hung up.

"What's going on?" Faith asked. "Is someone in my family sick? Hurt? DEAD?!"

I stared at her. "No, no, and what? Listen, Logan Hayes got hurt. Badly. And I need to go help Brooke watch him and Brianna, on top of you. So let's go. Now."

I had never spoken like that to anyone before, so Faith got the message. She stuck her sandwich in a plastic bag, set it down next to the note I was writing, and headed out to the shed, where they keep their bikes.

We hopped on the bikes and pedaled as fast as we could to Erin's house. I ran and knocked on the door. A teary-eyed seven-year-old answered. I walked inside.

"It's okay, Brianna. Brooke and I are going to make Logan feel better, and Faith is here to keep you company. Faith, why don't you two go upstairs to Erin's room? I'll go find Logan."

Well, it wasn't hard. He was screaming at the top of his lungs. I found him rocking back and forth in the living room, clutching his knee. Brooke was putting pressure on it to keep it from bleeding too badly. When she tried to stand up, he screamed louder.

"I'll go make the calls," I said as I started toward the kitchen.

First I called Brooke's mom, who's a nurse, and she said she'd be right over. Then I called my dad to tell him I might be a little late. Then I called Logan's mom, who also turned around right then and there to come home.

It was a very interesting job. First Brooke's mom showed up, then an ambulance showed up, then Logan's mom showed up, and ended up paying Brooke so everyone could go home.

As soon as I got back to Jenna's house, I checked the clock. Four fifty-nine. As if on cue, the front door opened. I threw my note away and met Jenna and her brother in the foyer. Faith followed me.

"So, what happened while we were gone?" Jenna asked.

I smiled, shrugged, and left.

Chapter Two:

I was home twenty minutes later.

"Hi, Dad," I said as I passed him, heading for my room.

"Hey. How'd the job go?"

I sighed. "Well, let's just say it's a long story."

He nodded, as if to say he understood. "Yeah. I feel bad for Logan. That happened to me once, but I was in high school."

"Right. You fell on that tack."

He nodded again. "Your friends will be here soon, so go on upstairs."

"Okay." I ran up to my room and closed the door. No sooner had I done that than I heard the front door open, then footsteps bounding upstairs. My door opened. It was Jenna.

"Hey," she said, "What time is it?"

I looked at my digital clock, the one we always used to tell 'club' time. "Five twenty-four. You're not late."

"Good." I looked up. That hadn't been Jenna. Erin had appeared in my doorway.

Before long, Brooke showed up. We were ready to start.

As you probably know, Jenna Morris is my very, very best friend in the entire world. She says I'm hers. We've known each other since . . . well, since I got to America, really. Her mom and my dad dated for a while in college, and they stayed close friends, so when her mom found out he had a baby the same age as hers, they decided we were best friends. Jenna never knew her dad, though, but she had one. We're like one person sometimes, but other times . . . wow, are we different. Like family. Oh, and looks, of course. Like I said, at home, it's just me and Dad. No sisters. No brothers. No mom. Jenna has one older brother, Tyler, who's fourteen, and a mom. Then she has a step dad, Tim. Tim has two sons, Greg, who's sixteen, and Seth, who's thirteen. Then, of course, he has one daughter, Faith. Plus, the one time Jenna moved was from her old house across from mine to a new, bigger house across town, not halfway across the globe. About the house, no one in their family is really "rich", so there are a couple down sides to the house. For one thing, Greg is the only one with his own room. And, they couldn't afford a house with a garage. Other than that, it's perfect.

As far as looks, I have, as I said, black hair and brown eyes. I'm also really bony, because I'm a picky eater. Jenna has long, wavy brown hair and brown eyes. Plus, she looks like a normal person who eats three meals a day, and sometimes she makes me look like a spaghetti person. Oh, and as opposed to my "not quite white, not quite black" skin, she's so light-skinned she looks like a china doll.

Now on to the parts that make us one. For one thing, we have the same goal in life – to help people. Don't get me wrong, Brooke and Erin love helping people too, but they have other plans for adulthood, which is why they jumped at the chance to be members of the CC. Not us. And we're smart in different ways than people expect. For instance, Jenna's grades aren't always great, but she loves science, and would even like to help people when she grows up by inventing new medicines. I get good grades, but I love going in my dad's study and researching places to see what people out there are like. I know that's not as exciting as Jenna, but who cares?

The cool thing is, even though we've each got our own thing, we love the other person's thing. We could talk about science and chemicals for hours one day, then spend hours talking about Asia (our favorite foreign continent). We used to pretend we were on different continents or in a lab. Oh, and we're not the most mature people in the world. Kids in our grade already like boys (even Brooke and Erin), but we aren't interested. And we don't care much about fashion. I like girly things, and she likes casual things, but we couldn't get into one of those endless "what should I wear" conversations. We like what we like. That's that.

Oh, and Jenna is a weird personality mix. She's outgoing, like me (only not as much), but she's also sensitive. She doesn't cry nonstop, but if something's bothering her, she doesn't try to hide it. She'll cry. But she can usually calm down long enough to tell you what's wrong. Then she'll cry until she's okay. And I'm not trying to be offensive. It's the truth. She says so herself sometimes. She's also nice. Really nice. If she doesn't know someone who got hurt, she'll help them anyway. She doesn't care what kind of looks they give her. And she's polite. She's like one of those 'ladies' from old times flipped around a little bit. But she's really great to be with.

Then there's Brooke McCully. Like Jenna, Brooke has lived in New Jersey all her life. She has one sister, Brianna, who you've met. Her parents are together and happy. She's very smart, but outgoing. Her mom and dad were worried about her when she started school, afraid she wouldn't be able to make any friends because she's African-American. But then she met Erin, who became her very best friend. Soon she met Jenna and me, and that's how the four of us became friends.

Plus, when we met Brooke, she was almost as outgoing as me. Then, being best friends with Erin, she grew a little less outgoing, but she's still plenty outgoing. She's kind too. Not quite as kind as Jenna, but I don't think a walking manners book could beat her. Also, like Jenna, she's polite (again, not as polite, but as close as any human could get). She was also the first one to start liking boys and clothes. And soon after that, Erin did too. I think boys are stupid and immature (Jason = Exhibit A, Michael = Exhibit B), but it's their business.

Anyway, Brooke has black hair that reaches down barely below her ears and brown eyes (we're a brown-eyed group). She's a little short for our age, but taller than her best friend. She's also the only one in the club who's allowed to get her ears pierced, and only once. EVER.

Oh, well. She doesn't mind. She thinks it'll hurt, so she only wants it to be done one time.

On to Erin. Erin Hayes. She's different. She's shy. Not as shy as she was before she met Brooke, but still shy. But she's really creative. She lives with her Mom and her two brothers, Logan, who's eight, and Caleb, who's fifteen. Her parents got divorced when she was four, and so right after her fifth birthday she moved from Florida to New Jersey. She always says, "I may look like I belong here, but I'm a Florida girl at heart." What's worse is that she moved in the wintertime, so not only did she have to adjust, she had to adjust FAST!

Erin's great for a couple main reasons. One, she had to live with one parent (like me) growing up, but she did have another parent out there that she couldn't see. And she's fine with that. She says if her dad wants to see her, he should keep in touch. I don't think I could do that, but she's great about it. She loves her mom, and she's open to maybe getting a step dad one day. And second, she's more than she seems. People say I'm more than I seem, but not as much as Erin. She's shy, but she's also smart and creative. She wants to learn how to make her own clothes someday.

Have you ever heard the expression "dumb blonde"? That's the part no one can understand about Erin. She's smart, but she's the girl stereotype, with blonde hair and blue eyes. Erin's another thin person, not because she doesn't eat, but because she doesn't eat very many sweets. Her mom, grandma, and big brother have a blood sugar problem, so she likes to watch her eating habits so she doesn't get it. She always dresses in great outfits. She keeps up with the latest trends and then sets her own.

Now for the CC (**C**ommunity **C**lub). I started it myself. It was kind of just a random idea I had that I wanted to go through with. And it was recently, too. I'd thought of it in February, and we started it in April. The only people in it are the four of us, which is good, because then we can goof off in our own way. We all have offices. I'm president, because I thought of it. That just means that I'm the one who runs the meetings, which I take very seriously. The meetings are at my house because it's at a good spot for everyone to get to (especially me).

The vice-president is Jenna. That just means she can run a meeting if I can't come (she also finds a replacement setting). It also means she sometimes brings snacks for us to eat while we work.

Brooke is our secretary. She keeps track of when we're free to work on projects in a special notebook (which we call our club's official calendar).

Erin has the job of treasurer. She keeps a record of how much we have, and each week she collects $2 from each of us.

Our meetings are Monday, Wednesday, and Friday from 5:30 to 6:30, which sometimes interferes with jobs we get around the neighborhood, but sometimes people leave early for that.

Back to that Friday. It was the beginning of the month, which meant it was time to work on a new project. I stared at my clock until it turned to five thirty.

"Okay. This Community Club meeting is officially started. Erin?"

"Dues day!" She passed an envelope around the room, and everyone gave her their money. "We now have . . .

fourteen dollars and seventy-three cents. That's enough to start our next project. What should we do?"

The phone rang, and a second later, Dad came in. "Phone for you, girls." We hadn't gotten a phone call during a meeting, so we weren't sure who should answer it. In the end, Jenna did.

"Community Club, this is Jenna . . . uh-huh . . . . wow . . . . okay . . . . so what should we do for her . . . . okay . . . . I'll get right back to you . . . . 'bye."

She turned around. "That was Mrs. McCully. I think she has our next project. She says a girl in our school named Cynthia Hale was just admitted into the hospital with leukemia. She's in fifth grade, like us, and needs money for treatments her parents can't pay for."

"What's gonna happen if she doesn't get the treatments?" Erin asked nervously.

Jenna gulped. "She might die." We were surprised. We knew you could die of cancer, but we didn't know it could happen when you were so young.

"What does leukemia affect, exactly?" Jenna asked.

"My mom told me once that it has something to do with your blood cells and the number of cells you have in your body," Brooke said.

We called Brooke's mom back and told her we'd do it. She gave us some ideas about what to do, and Brooke wrote them down:

Lemonade Stand
Fundraiser
Garage Sale
Donation Box

More than one of the above

We ruled out the donation box because we didn't think people would take us seriously. We were too young to have a fundraiser by ourselves, so this is what it looked like after ten minutes of talking:

Lemonade Stand
~~Fundraiser~~
Garage Sale
~~Donation Box~~
~~More than one of the above~~

"We could make more money with a garage sale," Erin pointed out. "But that would take more time than the other one, so I'm not sure if we'd be able to finish by the end of the month."

"Sure we could," Jenna said. "If we put our minds to it. We have to help her."

I nodded. "And we could pool our junk to make more money."

"Yeah," Brooke added. "And one of us can run a lemonade stand while we sell things, in case people get hot."

We all nodded. "Great," I said. "But where can we hold it? My garage isn't big enough."

"I flat out don't have one," Jenna said.

"We could use my garage," Brooke offered. "It's a double with plenty of room and it's basically right off of the kitchen for the lemonade stand. Plus, my mom was the one who brought it up, so I have a feeling she'll be okay with it."

"Okay, then. Madame President?" Erin teased.

I smirked, but I was smiling. "Okay!"

Brooke opened our calendar. "This'll take major planning. Today's the second, right? We can hold it on the 31st. Let's see. Tomorrow we have time to go to the hospital and see her, then next weekend we can put up fliers, then the weekend after that we can pool our junk. Starting on the 19th we can organize the junk, then on the 24th we can visit again, and the week of the 25th we can price. Sound good?"

We slowly nodded, since most of us never understand her when she gets into something.

"Let's call parents to see who can take us to the hospital tomorrow," Erin suggested.

"Mom's got work," Brooke countered.

"Dad's car is too small to hold us without someone in the front seat, which is illegal," I put in.

"Tim's got work, but Mom is free," Jenna said.

"My mom has brother duty tomorrow," Erin added.

"I'll call Mrs. Morris." I picked up the phone and dialed her number. "Hello. It's me, Aubrey," I said when she picked up. We talked for about five more minutes, then hung up.

"She said yes!" I announced.

We squealed.

"Okay," Jenna said. "Should we make the fliers now or sometime next week?"

"Maybe sometime next week," Brooke said. "That way we have something to do."

"Yeah," Erin agreed. "That way right now we could make cards for her." We did. In the end, mine looked like this:

Get Well!

Dear Cynthia,

I heard you had leukemia, and I can't imagine how bad that has to be. I'm sorry. My friends and I are going to help you. We will pay two visits to you this month, and then we'll have a surprise for you next month. I hope you get well.

Your Friend,
Aubrey

Jenna's looked like this (much neater than mine):

Get Well!

Dear Cynthia,

I heard about your cancer. You must be upset. Being that sick at our age must be extremely scary. Get well.

Sincerely,
Jenna Morris

Brooke's note looked like this:

Get Well Soon!

Dear Cynthia,

I'm sorry about your sickness. I know I'd be really scared if

I were you. Hold on tight, though. I think I (well, and my friends) can help.

                                        Signed,
                                        Brooke

And Erin didn't write one. She was going to be talking, so she'd just say everything we wanted to say.

I looked at the clock. Six twenty-eight. "Okay, everybody," I announced. "We'll meet at Jenna's house tomorrow. What time?"

"Well, it's a half hour drive there," Erin said. "What about noon?"

We agreed, and the meeting ended.

I ran downstairs for dinner and told Dad the news.

"That's great, hon," he said. "You're really helping that little girl."

I nodded. "Yeah. Dad, do grown-ups get leukemia?"

"Unfortunately, yes, they do. Everybody has a chance of getting it."

I frowned. "How much of a chance? Daddy, you gotta give me more than that."

"Well, okay. One sad fact is that some extreme treatments have just as much a chance of killing people as they do saving them. My uncle died from leukemia, my cousin had leukemia once and almost died, and you know my sister, Margo?"

"Aunt Margo. Sure. And Uncle Tom."

He nodded. "Well, your cousin Rachel was the second time they had a baby. The first time was about ten years before you were even born. The baby came, got all the way to second grade, then got leukemia, and died the next year. I'm sorry, Aubrey. I've known lots of people who died because of leukemia."

"So how many people do you know who survived?"

"Two. But I've heard of more."

I started to cry. "What if Cynthia doesn't make it?"

My dad walked with me into the living room and we sat on the couch. "She will."

"How do you know?"

He smiled. "Because I've heard a heck of a lot more stories about kids surviving than adults. Plus, she's got nurses, her parents, and four very special little girls who I know will not let her die."

I tried to smile back, but I couldn't. "You really think we can do it?"

"No. I know you can. You girls are more devoted to this stuff than anyone else I have ever met."

"What else can we do?"

He thought for a minute.

"Well?"

"You can visit her more often than you're planning to."

I frowned. "What good will that do?" I asked, putting my head on his shoulder.

"Well, think about it. What's the most important thing to have when you're that ill?"

"Doctors who know what they're doing?"

"No." He laughed. "Hope."

"Hope?"

He nodded. "Hope. If she gives up on living, her body will stop doing the work it needs to do to keep her alive. And having friends who stop and give her confidence and support, she'll have a lot better chance."

I thought about that. "Okay. We'll do it."

I went to bed that night with good thoughts, but I had no idea what was going to pop in my mind next.

Chapter Three:

"Augh!" I woke up in the night, panting. I didn't know what had awakened me, but I remembered having a terrible dream about . . . about . . . that's the part I couldn't quite remember. I screamed when I woke up. My dad came running.

"What happened, Aubrey? Are you okay?"

I shook my head. "What time is it?"

He checked my clock. "Three thirty, why?"

I took a deep breath and didn't say anything.

"What happened?"

"I don't know," I said, trying to catch my breath. "I just remember having this horrible dream, but I don't know what about. I know it had something to do with you, but that's it. What do you think?"

"I think it's the middle of the night and you need some more rest. But, I guess if it's really bothering you, we can go make some tea and talk about it."

I nodded and followed him downstairs to the kitchen. While he made the tea the dream kind of came back to me. "Hey, Dad?"

"Hmm?"

"Where would I go if something happened to you?"

He turned around and looked at me. "What?"

"If you died, who would I live with?" I repeated.

"I don't know. You'd probably go to the Morris'. You know, I have that paperwork in the garage, I think. Why do you ask?"

I shrugged. "Well, you said you've heard of more kids surviving cancer than adults, and you've never gotten married, and I don't even know what would happen if you got put into the hospital!"

Dad sighed. "What are you really asking me, Aubrey?"

I started crying. "I don't know."

"Do you wish you knew your real parents?"

I shook my head. "No. I just – I don't know."

"Well, when you do know, I'm ready to talk to you about it. For now, why don't you go back to bed?"

I nodded, and went upstairs to bed.

The next morning, I felt something pushing me. "Noooo."

"Yeeees!" I heard my dad say. I sat up.

"What time is it?"

"Ten fifty-three. Time to get up. I need to talk to you."

I sighed. Usually 'I need to talk to you' means I'm in Deep Trouble. "Okay."

I dragged myself into the bathroom and took a shower, then went back to my room to pick out an outfit. I ended up wearing a pink T-shirt and jeans, then I put on white sneakers and pulled my hair back into a ponytail. When I got downstairs, I smelled pancakes. Yum. My favorite.

"What's the occasion?" I asked when I saw Dad putting chocolate chips in my pancake (not to mention he wasn't just using Eggo, like he usually does).

He smiled. "I have some news."

"Good news or bad news?" I asked.

He shrugged. "It's the kind of news that could go either way, depending on your perspective."

I dropped my fork. "We aren't moving, are we?"

He chuckled. "No, we're not moving." He sat down. "I'm not going to beat around the bush (I gave him a Look). Okay, I am. I've been thinking about what you said last night, and I want to ask you something."

"Yeah?"

"Do you ever wish you had a mom?"

I thought about that. Sometimes I did, actually. "Yeah, sometimes. I just didn't want to tell you - "

"Cause you thought I would be offended. Well, I'm not. And I thought that's what you'd say, so . . ."

I was bouncing off the walls. "Yeah?"

He shrugged. "Never mind."

"Daaaaaaad!" I whined. "Come on, what?"

"Maybe you won't like it."

"Maybe I will."

He shook his head. "No, I don't think you will. It's too much to ask at this age."

"Come on, Dad. Tell me."

"Okay. I'm going to start dating again."

I was shocked. "Do you mind repeating that for me?

I don't think I heard right – Did you just say you want to start *dating*?"

Dad laughed. "Yes I did. I think you need a woman in the house. Am I getting the impression that you don't like it?"

"No, no. I think having a mom would be great, but on two conditions."

"What?"

I set my fork down. "One, I don't want to call her my step mom, because I've never had a mom in America, so she'll be my real mom."

"Okay."

"And two, I like being an only child, so no step siblings."

He solemnly nodded. "Got it."

"So," I said, picking up my fork, "How are you planning to meet people?"

He shrugged. "Around town. I don't like blind dates and Internet dating. I'd rather meet someone in person."

I smiled. "I can't wait to have a mom!"

Chapter Four:

"Eek!" It was noon. My friends and I were on the way to the hospital to see Cynthia. I had just told them about my dad's decision, and my conditions.

"If I were you, I'd ask to stay an only child too," Jenna said. "I should've thought of that."

"What would you do with Tyler?" Erin questioned.

She shrugged. "Marry somebody with a big dog. Maybe it'd eat him."

We laughed. "Good luck," Brooke said.

"Did you mean what you said?" Jenna asked.

"What do you mean?"

"When you said you weren't upset? Did you mean it?"

I nodded. "Sure I meant it. She'd be my mom! I've never had one. I'm pretty psyched!"

Erin changed the subject. "Are you guys excited to meet Cynthia?"

We nodded. "Yeah," I said. "I think we could become friends."

"Well," Brooke said. "My mom said she's been fighting this for over a year now, so we should expect her not to be as enthusiastic about her getting well as we are."

I nodded. "My dad said hope is the most important thing for her to have." I explained it like he had.

"My parents said the same thing," Jenna agreed.

Erin spoke up. "What if she's given up altogether?"

We laughed. "I don't think it's gone that far," Brooke said. "Although, my mom isn't one of her nurses. But she's eleven, so I don't think she wants to give up on high school, college, and life."

We pulled up in front of the hospital and got out. Mrs. Morris walked in with us. We found the information desk and the four of us walked up to it, leaving Mrs. Morris in a chair. I was elected to speak to the woman, which was okay with me, because she looked nice, with light brown hair and dark green eyes, and a real smile, not like the fake smiles you see on commercials.

"Hello, how may I help you girls?" she said.

"We're looking for Cynthia Hale," I replied.

"Relation?"

"What?"

She smiled. "How are you related to her?"

"We're her friends," I said. "We're the Community Club. We help people, and one of my friends' mom works here. She told us about Cynthia, and we'd like to help her family pay for more chemo. We thought we'd come here and visit first."

She nodded. "So you haven't met this girl yet?"

I shook my head. "No."

"Can I have the name of the worker, and what she does?"

Brooke stepped up. "Sandra McCully, nurse." (I think she'd done this before), "she works in children's ICU and in the baby nursery."

"Is she here today? Working?"

We nodded.

The woman called Mrs. McCully, who told her yes, we had permission to go visit Cynthia, then she called Cynthia's main nurse to make sure it wasn't a bad time, and then she gave us the room number.

"Thank you," I said. The lady smiled.

We rode the elevator up to the fifth floor, and followed the signs that led to the cancer waiting room. There we found a man with blonde hair sitting with his wife on a bench. We approached them. Brooke's turn to speak.

"Are you Mr. and Mrs. Hale?" she asked. They nodded.

"Who are you?" the man countered.

Brooke explained the club to the man, who smiled. I guess no one our age had come to see her. While Mrs. Hale talked to the nurse, Mr. Hale reminded us that the first chemo treatment their daughter had made her lose her hair, so we were prepared. He also told us that she had a bandana to cover her head, because she was embarrassed to show it. Then the nurse led us in.

"This is Cynthia," the nurse told us, gesturing to a girl with dark brown eyes who was sitting on the bed.

"Go away!" Cynthia screamed.

"Now, now, Cynthia," the nurse said patiently. "These girls are here to help you."

She shook her head. "No one can help me, let alone kids."

The nurse wished us good luck and left us alone. I started explaining the club and she calmed down a little, then Jenna pulled out the cards and gave them to Cynthia while Erin got up some nerve and starting talking.

Cynthia smiled. "This is really nice of you guys, not making fun of me because I'm bald, but it's no good."

"What do you mean?" Brooke asked.

She shrugged. "I'm gonna die, and I know it."

I don't know about my friends, but that made my heart sink to my stomach. "You can't give up."

"Yes, I can. My parents can't afford the treatment I need to make me better, and without it I can't live."

I shook my head. "No. No. Without chemo you can live for a while longer. We're going to raise money to help you."

She laughed, then sighed. "That's the nicest thing anyone has ever done for me, but we have to pay $15,000 up front or they won't do it, and insurance will only give us $10,000. We have a little over $4500, but we need, like, $475 by June 20th or they're going to dismiss me. No offense, but I don't think kids our age could make that much that fast."

I smiled at my friends. "Let's make a deal, Cynthia."

She cocked her head. "I'm listening."

"We'll try as hard as we can to raise the money *if* you promise us one thing."

"What?"

"You have to promise that you will never say 'I'm gonna die' until we give you the money. Deal?"

She nodded. "Deal. Now, can you tell me about yourselves?"

We laughed. I went first. I told her I was adopted, I never had a mom, I live with my dad and no siblings, and that my dad is starting to date.

"That's awesome, and you're Aubrey?"

I nodded. "Aubrey Elizabeth Addison. Who next?"

"You," she said, pointing to Jenna.

Jenna told her about her step family, her wish for a dog to eat her brother, and her house.

"Aubrey, Jenna," Cynthia repeated, pointing to us. "This is like one of those games where you add something but you have to remember everything before that."

We laughed, then it was Brooke's turn. She told Cynthia about her sister, her parents, and her wish for a pet.

"Aubrey, Jenna, Brooke."

Erin went last. She talked about her brothers, her mom, the divorce, and Florida.

"Aubrey, Jenna, Brooke, Erin," Cynthia said. "Okay, my turn. Well, I'm the oldest of nine kids – yeah, nine – and we live right next to Erin now that I really look at her, so I guess kind of behind Aubrey? Um, oh, I usually have wavy red hair, but my parents say it might grow back a different color. I have four sisters and four brothers, and two of my sisters, McKayla and McKenzie, are identical twins. They even dress alike, and their room is symmetrical. They do that on purpose so no one can tell them apart, and it works. My mom made them get bracelets so people outside our family can tell them apart. The weird part is, the secret has to do more with looks than personality. They're almost one, except Kenzie gets better grades." She told us some more about herself, and then Mrs. Morris came in and said we had to leave.

"Wait!" We turned around. Cynthia was calling us. "Do you guys baby-sit?"

We nodded. We told her our numbers, then left.

Chapter Five:

"Come on, Dad! Let's go, let's go!" I called. It was Sunday, the day after our visit, and Erin and I were supposed to baby-sit Cynthia's little brothers and sisters while her parents visited her in the hospital. Dad had said he wanted to come with me to meet her parents, so that's why I was standing at the foot of the steps, calling him.

"I'm coming," he said. A moment later we were walking out the back door.

As we approached the house, I said, "Dad, Mrs. Hale said we could knock on the back door and someone will let us in, okay?"

He nodded. "Okay."

I looked down to make sure I looked okay. This was my outfit: a yellow tank; a blue and yellow baby tee; a faded miniskirt; white leggings; blue sequin flip-flops (I was much more dressed up than usual). Erin answered the door. Her outfit was: a pink cami; a tan crop jacket;

a white mini skirt (told you my outfit was more like her style); white sneakers.

"Oh, hi, guys. Come on in. Mr. Hale was just about to introduce me to the kids. He's making sure the twins haven't switched bracelets." I giggled, then let her lead me into the living room to wait.

A few minutes later Mr. Hale appeared in the doorway. He cleared his throat. "Welcome, girls." He lined the kids up in the living room. They all had red hair and brown eyes. He started with the oldest and worked his way down. "This is Katherine, or Katie, and she's ten. This is Justin; he's nine. This is McKayla, and this is McKenzie, or Kayla and Kenzie; they're eight. This is Adam; he's seven. This is Kevin; he's six. This is Lucas; he's five. And this little girl is Grace; she's four. Let's see, it's nine thirty right now, so I'm gonna go. The kids – you know what, I left a note on the kitchen counter. Love you, kids. Be good to the girls. Oh, and Katie will tell you the secret to telling the twins apart. 'Bye." He talked to my dad, then left.

"Okay," I said. Grace started crying. Erin picked her up. I continued. "I'm Aubrey, and this is my friend Erin. We're friends of Cynthia's. Can one of you show me where the kitchen is?"

Katie stepped in front of her siblings. "I can. Follow me. Erin, you, too."

We followed her into the kitchen. I looked around. "Where's the note?"

"There is no note. He does this every time. He forgets the note. I'm the note. Okay, Grace needs to be kept busy so she doesn't realize our family of ten, at the moment, has decreased to a family of eight with two baby-sitters.

Keep an eye on Lucas, he tries to do things he isn't big enough to do. The twins' secret is their mole. Kayla's is above her mouth, and Kenzie's is below it. Um, oh, I'm a big help, and Justin thinks he is, but he's not." She gave us some more instructions, then showed us around the house, managing to get everybody in the rec room.

Kayla walked up to me. "Dad asked us to make get-well cards for Cynthia, but I know that she might die. Last time we visited her, she said something about never making it. I think she gave up for good."

I smiled. "I don't think so. See, she promised us she'd hang on for a while longer, so I wouldn't be too worried about that. I do think get-well cards are a good idea. They might help her feel better. I think her biggest concern is that a lot of kids at school make fun of her because she's bald."

"She's not bald."

Oops.

Kevin walked up to me. "We're *bored,*" he said.

I looked to Erin for help, but she was busy, so I said, "Who wants to play hide and seek?"

Cries of "Me, me!", "I'm counting first!", "No, I am!", and the ever popular "Waaaaaaah!" filled the room. I held my hand up to keep them quiet.

"Okay. Here are the rules. We're playing upstairs and only upstairs. If something gets broken, the game is over. Katie will be It first. Whoever she finds first is It next. Grace and Lucas need a buddy, whom I will choose. Deal?" They nodded. "Okay. Justin is Lucas' partner, Katie is Grace's. Oh, and if someone yells 'Come out, come out, come out', you come out. People count in the rec room, and no pushing or hitting, especially by the stairs. Understand?"

More nods. Everyone took off except Katie and Grace, who stayed behind to count. Erin and I sat on the couch to supervise and talk.

I told her what Kayla had said about her sister not being bald.

"Maybe they never actually got to see her," Erin suggested.

I nodded. "Maybe. But she seemed pretty confident. I don't know what they did, but I have a feeling if they did get to see her, she didn't look like she did yesterday."

"What do you mean?"

I shrugged. "I don't know. Like maybe she had a wig on that looked like it was her hair. I know it's far-fetched, but, hey, it makes more sense than them not - "

"Aaaaaah!"

Erin and I glanced at each other, then took off running. "What was that?" I asked.

Justin laughed. "Nothing. The girls yelled 'come out', so we jumped out of the linen closet, where we were hiding, and yelled 'Boo!' It scared Katie."

"Did not."

"Did so."

"Did not."

"Uh-huh."

"Uh-uh."

"Uh-huh."

"No."

"Yes."

"No."

"*Yes.*"

"NO!"

"YES!"

I stood between them, noticing we were missing four kids. "Okay, that's enough. Both of you. I want you to go to your rooms until you can treat each other with respect. There are eight kids in the house at the moment and you two are the oldest ones, so act like it!" I yelled. Luckily, I knew what I was saying. It turns out that they had to separate right there to go to their rooms.

"You sound like our mother," Justin said.

Once that had been settled, I turned to Erin. "We're missing a few people."

"Yeah. Did you see them when we came in here?"

I shook my head. "Maybe for a split second, but not for long."

We heard giggling from downstairs. We ran down the steps two at a time and followed the giggles into the dining room, but couldn't find anyone. Then we heard them again and found ourselves in the family room. Next they led us into the master bedroom.

I stopped dead in my tracks. "Do you hear anything?" I asked.

"Nope."

"Exactly. Where did they go?"

Erin sighed.

The giggles were in the living room. There was a knock on the door. The two of us ran to get it.

"Wait," I said. "Who's the oldest person in the group we're missing?"

Erin thought about that, and her eyes grew wide. She turned to me. "The twins."

I nodded. "That's what I thought. They can definitely

figure out how to trick us and get their brothers and sisters involved. So I'm gonna answer the door, just in case. And maybe you should block the staircase, but not directly."

"Got it."

We made our way casually into the foyer, and I answered the door. When no one was there, I stepped outside to check, and heard Erin say, "Gotcha!"

I whipped around. Standing in front of her were the six youngest kids in the Hale family. "That wasn't funny. Who thought of that?" Everyone pointed at Kenzie.

"Well," she said, "I can't take all the credit. Kayla helped."

I grunted. "I don't care who helped. Who all was in on it? Just you guys?"

"No," Kayla replied. "Justin and Katie's fight was a distraction so we could come downstairs without you noticing us. When did you figure it out?"

"When I realized you two were the oldest missing kids, I knew you were up to something."

She shrugged. "Okay. What time is it?"

I checked my watch. "Eleven thirty, why?"

"Becca Anderson down the street said we could come over to her house at one."

I raised my eyebrow. "We?"

"Yeah. Kenzie and me."

"Okay - "

"We can go?"

I shook my head. "No. Your sister didn't say anything about anyone going to a friend's house, so you're all staying here until your parents get back tonight."

Grace started crying. "Where are Mommy and

Daddy?" (Although, through tears it sounded more like, "Wa Ma a' Daaaa-y?").

I picked her up and comforted her, then turned back to the twins, who were now the only kids there (the rest of them had gone upstairs to be kept in the rec room by Erin). "No one is going anywhere," I repeated. "Your parents said they'd be back around four thirty, so after that you can go to Becca's house. Until then, eight kids are in this house."

"Actually," Kenzie said. "Technically, that's saying we can go, because you two are kids, so there's ten right now, and minus the two of us, you're good to go. 'Bye."

I stared at her. "Like I said, no one is leaving until your mom and dad get back."

"Fine." The girls huffed up to their room.

Fortuately, the rest of the job was uneventful, at least compared with our little hide and seek adventure.

When I got home, I found Dad in the kitchen wearing a tux.

"Wow, you look nice," I said.

He looked down. "Oh, this. Yeah, I went to the grocery store while you were gone yesterday and - "

"The potatoes asked you to dress up while fixing them?"

He laughed. "No. I met this woman, Melissa Howard, and we're going out tonight."

"Wow. You met her at the grocery?"

"No. After that, at the post office. Well, actually, we aren't *going* anywhere. I invited her here to have dinner with us."

I raised my eyebrows. "Us?"

He nodded.

I shook my head. "I'll meet her, but I'm pretty sure the definition of 'date' is you and Melissa, not you and Melissa, with me."

"Well, then. She'll be here . . . well, any minute now."

Ding-dong.

"That's her," Dad said. He ran to meet her (if you've ever seen a thirty-five-year-old man in a tux run, you know I was on the floor from laughing so hard).

I closed the door in the foyer (just in case). A couple seconds later, the door opened. A woman with a huge smile on her face who had brown hair and blue eyes walked in with Dad.

"Hi," I said.

"Hi," she replied, looking at me then Dad then back at me. "You must be Aubrey. Um . . . well . . . "

"I'm adopted from Japan, since Dad has never married. Hoing ha!"

Melissa laughed. "You're right, Mark (my dad). She is funny."

"I got it from him. Spend eleven years with him and you're telling bad jokes left and right."

More laughter.

"She's kidding," my dad said.

I nodded.

There was a silence. Finally, Dad spoke to me. "Melissa is twenty-nine. That's only eighteen years older than you, Aubs."

"Yup. Is that a good thing?"

He nodded. "I thought so, because then you could not only have a woman around, but at the same time, she's young enough to do fun things with you that don't quite qualify as *father*-daughter stuff."

I giggled. "Okay."

"You two talk," Dad said. "I'll go finish making dinner."

"So," Melissa said. "This is a pretty big house for just you and your dad, huh?"

I nodded. "Yeah, but I'm pretty sure my best friend Jenna has part ownership of the place by now. You'll be seeing a lot of her if you and my dad get married." I slapped my hand over my mouth.

Melissa laughed. "It's okay. I know this sounds really corny to you, but I've always wanted to meet someone and know he's who I want to be with. Even when I was your age."

"And you think my dad's that person?"

"I don't know, but when I saw him . . . there was this feeling . . ." Her voice trailed off. "Oh, well. Like I said, this is probably corny - "

"You know," I said. "When I got home from a baby-sitting job today my dad was happier than I can ever remember."

She smiled. "Well, I hope things work out between us."

"Yeah," I replied. Me, too."

Chapter Six:

Dad walked in. "Dinner's almost ready, ladies. Hey, Aubs, why don't you show Melissa around the house?"

"Okay, Dad," I agreed. I really liked Melissa, I could tell she really liked me, and Dad and Melissa really liked each other. It was perfect.

I pointed to the door on her left. "That's Dad's office. He works here so he can be with me. Where do you work?"

"I work for an Internet company, so I get to work at home, too."

I showed her the rest of the first floor.

"Okay," she said. "I didn't see any stairs."

I giggled.

"What's so funny?"

"Well, when we were talking about how much you like my dad, they were right in front of you."

I showed her where, and she started laughing, too.

We went upstairs. I showed her the master bedroom. She was impressed with the closet (Dad was right; I did need someone to share my interest in his closet).

"Wow, this is big," she said.

I nodded. "It's almost bigger than my bedroom."

"Speaking of which, where is that?"

"Oh, follow me."

I led her across the hall into my bedroom.

"It's nice," she said.

"Yeah. It's been my room my entire life – well, except the first six weeks I spent in Japan."

"Six weeks?" Melissa asked. "Wow. You were adopted that early?"

"Yeah. I don't remember Japan, but Dad says one day, we might go there on vacation. But I don't care."

"This is . . . personalized." We were in the guest room. "Are you sure you're an only child?"

I nodded. "This is where Jenna always sleeps."

"During sleepovers?" Melissa looked at me skeptically.

I giggled. "No. Her mom and step dad have business trips together, and she stays here."

"Oh." She smiled at me. "You know, even if I don't marry your dad, we can still hang out. In fact, why don't we do something this weekend, just the two of us? What do you say?"

"Um, maybe. Can I call my friends first?"

"Why?"

I explained the club to her and what we were working on.

"Wow. You know, I really hope more than ever that things work out, because I've always wanted a daughter, but a daughter who loves to help other people? That's more than I could dream of. Go ahead."

I went into my dad's room and called Jenna.

"Hello?"

"Hi, Jenna."

"Hi, Aubrey. What's up?"

"My dad got a girlfriend."

She squealed.

"I know. She really likes him, he really likes her, and I really like her, too. She doesn't baby me like I was afraid she might. She's more like my friend. And that's why I called. We're doing the fliers on Saturday, right?"

"Yeah, but if you and your dad - "

"No, not my dad. This woman, Melissa, wanted to know if the two of us could do something together, but I didn't know."

She giggled. "In that case, we can do it on Sunday."

"Really?"

"Sure."

"Great."

"I'll call Brooke and Erin."

"Cool."

"Oh, and Aubrey?"

"Yeah?"

"My parents said there *is* another trip coming up, but just a weekend trip. It starts a week from Thursday and they'll be back the following Monday."

"'Kay. I'll ask my dad."

"Great! 'Bye!"

"Bye!"

I hung up and went back into the hall.

"It's okay. We're going to do the fliers on Sunday. So, what do you want to do?"

"Well, if it's okay with your dad, what if we drove into Glendale on Saturday and go to Lincoln Mall and go shopping, maybe get our nails done, unless you don't want to. Your dad told me you're not much into that."

I laughed. "That's because it's been just the two of us, so I've never actually gotten my nails done. And I like shopping."

"Okay, then. How about I pick you up at eleven, and we'll grab some lunch first. Sound good?"

"Yeah."

We walked downstairs together, then I went back to my room to work on some homework. As soon as I opened my math book (ick), the phone rang. I ran to it.

"Hello?"

"Hi."

"Hi? Who is this?"

"Wait, is this Aubrey Addison?"

"Yes. Who are you?"

The girl giggled. "It's me, Cynthia. How's the project going?"

"We'll put fliers up this weekend. How's the cancer going?"

"The same as it has been for the past eighteen months."

I sighed. "Well, hopefully we can raise enough money."

"Yeah."

There was a lull.

"Guess what?" I asked.

"What?"

"My dad met this lady at the post office yesterday, and they're downstairs having dinner."

"Really?"

"Really!"

"Do you think . . . ?"

"Uh-huh."

She squealed. "That is sooooo awesome. What's her name?"

"Melissa. She doesn't baby me, either. She really likes my dad, he likes her, and I like her. I'm so excited."

"You should be."

"And she invited me to go to the mall this weekend. On Saturday. And then on Sunday we'll go hang fliers up. Is that okay?"

"Totally. I know if I were you I'd want to make friends with my possible mother. So don't even worry about me. Worse case - "

"You die, I know. But that isn't gonna happen. We are working as hard as we can. We're gonna get you your chemo, whatever it takes!"

"You sound like an army general."

"Rah! Rah!"

"Too cheerleader."

"CHARGE!" I said. We burst into laughter.

"Wow."

"What?"

"I haven't had a conversation like this in almost two years."

"Really?"

"Yeah. Ever since I was diagnosed, I've been a crank. I just thought I was going to die, so there was no point in fighting it. I'm pretty sure you guys saved my life. Now that I know about you guys, I'm feeling a little better. Your dad was right."

I smiled. "Thanks. Just hearing that makes me know we'll do whatever it takes."

"You're welcome" I mean, I gotta help myself."

I giggled. "Yeah. Right."

"What?"

"Remember? You're the one who almost killed yourself."

"Oh, yeah. I . . . forgot."

"Uh-huh."

She laughed. "You're a great friend, Aubrey."

"Yeah. I know."

"So what are you doing with Melissa?"

"We're going to the mall in Glendale, and we're going to get our nails done. She'll pick me up at eleven so we'll get some lunch first."

"Sounds awesome. Wanna stop by?"

"Sure! I bet she'd love to meet you!"

"Well, I'd love to meet her, too."

I sighed. "Yeah. I think my dad and Melissa are experiencing love at first sight."

"That's so romantic."

"I know. It's great."

"Speaking of great, how were the eight little monsters today?"

I shrugged, even though I knew she didn't see it. "Well, they all turned against us."

"Tell me all about it. It might help later on. Let me guess. The twin devils thought of it."

"You bet. They staged a fight between Justin and Katie, then went downstairs and - "

"Giggled, then moved, then giggled again?"

"How'd you know?"

"They've done it before. Lucky there were two of you. I chased them around until my parents got home."

"When?"

"Thursday. Mom and Dad ran some errands, so I baby-sat for the twins, who were the only two home. They played that trick on me, and their distraction was when my doctor called me."

"Ugh."

"No kidding."

My dad stuck his head up the stairs (I was using the phone in the hallway) and asked, "Who's on the phone?"

"Cynthia Hale, that girl I was telling you about."

"Well, wrap it up."

"Okay."

I turned back to the phone. "I gotta go."

"Okay. My nurse is here anyway. 'Bye."

"Bye."

Melissa appeared with Dad.

"Hey, Melissa?" I said. "Would you like to visit my friend Cynthia in the hospital on Saturday?"

She smiled. "I'd love to."

Chapter Seven:

Saturday. I woke up at ten o' clock and went downstairs, humming. Dad gave me a Look. "What are you so happy about?" he asked.

"I'm just so excited Dad. I really like Melissa."

He nodded. "So do I. Hey, Aubs?"

I looked up. That was his 'This Is Serious' tone. "Yeah?"

"I really think I love Melissa. So can I ask you a serious question?"

I nodded.

"If I said I wanted to marry her, what would you say?"

I smiled. "I'd say go for it. But isn't this a little sudden?"

He shook his head. "I don't know. It's just . . . we have so much in common, and she seems to really like me."

"Yeah, but love?"

"Can I ask you to snoop for me?"

I nodded. "Sure."

"Ask her what she'd say."

"Okay."

Ding-dong.

I stood up and went to the door. It was Melissa. "Wow," I said. "You're early."

"Yeah. I just couldn't wait."

"Neither could I. Let me just tell Dad we're going."

"Okay."

I stuck my head into the kitchen. "We're leaving."

"Have fun," he replied.

"We will." I walked out the front door with Melissa and we climbed into her car.

"It's only ten thirty," she pointed out. "Are you hungry, or did you just eat?"

I shook my head. "I'm kind of hungry. What about you?"

"Me, too. Where would you like to eat?"

I thought about that. "Ricky's." Ricky's is the best Mexican restaurant in New Jersey (probably).

"Mm. I love that place."

Speaking of which . . .

"Hey, Melissa?"

"Yeah?"

"Can I ask you something?"

"Sure."

"If my dad asked you to marry him, what would you say to him?"

She smiled. "I'd say yes."

My face lit up. "Really?"

"Heck, yeah!"

We pulled into Ricky's parking lot. Once we were seated, we started talking about stuff I'd never talked to my dad about. When it was time to leave, I spotted Brooke. "Hey!" I called.

"Hi." She looked pretty uncertain.

Finally I figured it out. "Oh, this is Melissa."

"Ohh. Hi! I'm Brooke, secretary of the CC."

Melissa smiled at her. "Hi." She turned to me. "I'm gonna go pay, okay?"

I nodded.

As soon as Melissa was out of earshot, Brooke said, "You're right, she does seem awesome. And nice."

"She is. And, I think my dad's going to propose! Isn't that great?"

"Yeah! I'm soooo happy for you."

Melissa walked back up to us. "Okay. 'Bye, Brooke."

"'Bye."

We got back in the car. "So," Melissa said. "do you want to pamper yourself and then go see Cynthia, or see Cynthia and then go pamper yourself?"

"I think pamper then visit, to save the best for last."

"That's sweet."

"Yeah."

The rest of the ride was quiet, unlike the mall. People were everywhere. I hadn't been to the mall in a long time, so I'd forgotten all about how crowded it is.

"So, where to first?" Melissa asked me.

"I don't know. Why don't we just look around a little? Besides, I didn't bring any money."

"Oh, I did. I brought some of my savings for my next vacation, which I canceled, and your dad gave me one hundred dollars to spend on you."

I giggled. "Good ol' Dad," I said.

"All right. Let's get shopping. I have a lot of money burning a hole in my pocket for this mall, and then some for the nail salon."

"Cool. Let's go."

We started walking around.

"Wow!"

I turned. "What?"

"Look!"

We were standing in front of a store called Lucky's. It was a girl's clothing store, and it'd just opened. I'd heard the clothes were expensive.

"Thirty percent off! Wanna go in?" Melissa asked.

I shrugged. "Why not?"

"That's the spirit! Come on!"

We walked into the store. It was filled with girls about my age and their moms. I started looking. Every so often I'd hear Melissa say, "That's cute!", "This would totally work for you", or "Oh, my gosh!".

"What do you think of this?" I asked, holding up a blue scoop neck baby tee.

"I love it! Let's find an outfit to go with it."

I let out a giggle. I wasn't pampering myself; Melissa was! I had to admit I liked it. "Okay," I agreed.

We looked some more until we found a white skirt, pink jeweled flip-flops, blue leggings, and a plaid hat.

"Do you wear dresses?"

I nodded. "Sometimes. Wh – Let's do it."

So, we went on a fancier outfit search. We came up with a black and white strappy floral dress (not as geeky as it sounds); a silver heel; a polka dot chain necklace; and a white button bag.

"Wow." I stared at our pile of stuff.

"So?" Melissa said. "Are you ready to buy this?"

"Sure."

She went up to the cashier and paid. When she got back, we left.

"Hey," Melissa said. "Why don't we head upstairs to get makeovers?"

I laughed. "Okay."

We went up the escalator to a store called *Sally's Boutique*. A woman named Monique guided me to another woman named Heather.

"Hi," she said.

"Hi."

"I'm the hair artist here. Your . . . adult over there said to put you through everything, so do you just want a trim to take away split ends?"

"No. I think I'd like a little bit of layering, if that's okay with Melissa."

"Well, she told us whatever you want, you get."

I smiled. "Okay. Then yeah, a trim and some layers."

She nodded. "Can do."

She put me in a chair and leaned it back until my neck was against a sink. She washed my hair, then said, "Okay. This mirror has been covered so you won't know what you look like until you're done. Is that all right?"

"Sure."

After that, she started clipping. And clipping. And clipping. After what seemed like two hours, she stood in front of me. "You look fantastic."

A woman named Margaret came next. She mixed up some stuff and turned it green, then put it on my face, avoiding my eyes. Then she put cucumber slices over my eyes. After fifteen minutes, she washed my face. "You look marvelous (by now I was quite curious)."

The next person to come was a woman named Jennifer. She moved me to a different chair, then sat on a stool by my feet, and started doing things with my feet. I was confused. When she was done, she led me to a table covered with stuff I couldn't recognize. She started my manicure (I'm not an idiot) by filing my nails. Then she put this gunk on that she said helped. I believed her. Finally they let me see myself.

"Whoa," I said. I looked really, really good. I looked down at my nails. They looked perfect! I thanked everyone (including Melissa), then we left.

In the car, Melissa asked, "What do you think?"

"I love it."

"Really?"

I nodded. "You better believe it. Thanks again."

"You're welcome. So, let's go meet this Cynthia."

"You are going to LOVE her, especially now that she isn't declaring she's going to die."

"Yeah. That would put a person in a bad mood, I think."

I laughed.

The rest of the ride was silent. When we got to the building, we walked up to the information desk. This time a man was sitting there.

"Cynthia Hale," I stated.

"Relation?"

"We're – well, I'm her friend."

He nodded. "And is there any other relation?"

"Sandra McCully," I said, remembering what Brooke had said last time we were here. "She's a nurse here. She works in ICU and the baby nursery. She's here working today." I explained the club. The man smiled.

"Ah," he said. "So you're one of the girls who was here last weekend? My friend, who was working that day, told me about you."

He gave me the room number and we headed for the elevators. "You handled that very professionally," Melissa said.

"Yeah. I just remembered what happened last time."

When we got to the right floor, I talked to Mr. and Mrs. Hale, then the nurse led me into Cynthia's room again. She knocked on the door. "Cynthia! They're here!"

The door was opened by another nurse. We walked inside.

"Hi, Aubrey!" Cynthia said to me.

I waved. "Hi!"

"What's up?" she asked, looking around her hospital room. "I don't see the woman."

I turned around. Melissa was standing where Cynthia couldn't see her. "Come on," I prodded.

She stepped out. "Hi, Cynthia. I'm Melissa."

"Hi, Melissa. How are you?"

"Pretty good. How are you?"

"Okay. That is, thanks to the CC."

I smiled. "It's true. We saved her life."

Cynthia nodded. "Thanks for coming and disrupting what looks like a fantastic day," she said, noticing my hair.

"Well, I figured I'd squeeze you in."

"Ugh!" she cried, pretending to be offended. We burst out laughing.

Our visit was short, though. Something started beeping. Doctors and nurses rushed in and shooed us out.

On our way home, Melissa said, "That girl must be having a hard time. I would hate to be in the middle of ten doctors trying to figure out what went wrong."

I just nodded. I knew the feeling.

Chapter Eight:

"We did it!" Jenna exclaimed. It was Sunday. We had just spent five hours (no kidding) driving all around New Jersey (okay, now I'm kidding) advertising our garage sale. We were now sprawled out on my bedroom floor, completely out of energy. Jenna and I were laying sideways on my bed, with our feet dangling off the edge. We were wet noodles dangling off the plate (okay, fine; I'm still kidding). Brooke was sitting backwards in my desk chair, resting her head on the top of it. Erin was laying on the floor, pretending to be dead.

"No kidding. What are we going to do now?" Brooke asked.

I shrugged. "We could follow Erin's example." We all looked at Erin (cue cricket sounds).

"I can't," Jenna said. "I have a nine-year-old calling."

Brooke pried her head from the chair. "Well, best of luck."

"Thanks," Jenna said, staring at our 'corpse'. "You too. I think she'd like being buried under that tree in her backyard."

We nodded. "Sure."

"Ouch! Aubrey! She keeps pulling my hair!"

I sighed. It was Monday afternoon, and I was sitting at the Hale's. Mr. and Mrs. Hale were at the hospital, Lucas, Kevin, and Adam were at T-ball practice and would spend the rest of the day with another baby-sitter, Justin was at a friend's house until his parents returned, and I don't think I need to tell you where Cynthia was. That left me with the twins, Grace, and Katie. Katie was complaining about Grace pulling her hair.

"Here," I said, picking up a coloring book and some crayons. "Give her these. I have to find your sisters."

Kayla and Kenzie weren't even in earshot, which meant they weren't playing their game of 'trick the baby-sitter'. "McKayla! McKenzie! Come here!" I started to get worried. What if they'd gone to a friend's house without telling me? What if they'd tried and a car ran over them? What if —

The phone rang. I picked it up.

"Hello, Hale residence."

Brooke's voice was at the other end. "Hi, Aubrey. My sister found two new playmates, and I think they might be yours, considering they look exactly alike. Plus, they look about a year older than her. Can you come get them, or should I bring them to you?"

I peered into Katie's room, where she was struggling to keep her sister from pulling her hair. "You better bring them here, and stay if you can."

She laughed. "Sure. We'll be right over." I hung up, then bumped into Katie, who was closing the door to her bedroom.

"Who was that?" she asked.

"My friend Brooke. You know about African-Americans, right?"

She nodded.

"Well, that's what her and her sister are, just to warn you so you aren't surprised."

"Okay," Katie replied. "Has she gotten that reaction before?"

I nodded. "All the time."

"Wow. It must be hard being her. I don't think there are any black – I mean, African fourth graders."

"Yeah. It is tough sometimes, especially when most of her friends are white."

"You aren't white, exactly."

"No, I'm not. I'm Asian. My dad's white, though."

"I don't follow."

I laughed. "Have you learned about adoption yet?"

"No. I know a tiny bit about it, but not much."

"Well, I was born in Japan."

"Wow."

"Tell me about it. Anyway, before I was born, my dad got in touch with an adoption agency. They asked him a whole bunch of questions about where he came from, how much he made, where he lived, stuff like that. Then he filled out a whole bunch of papers, and finally, long story minuscule, two weeks after my birth, he came to Japan, signed a bunch of papers, met me, and took me home. The end."

"Okay. What about your mom?"

"I don't really have a mom. My dad's never been married."

"Oh."

The doorbell rang. I answered it. It was Brooke, Brianna, and our two girls.

"Hello," I said to them. "What were you thinking?"

Kayla looked at the ground. "The truth is . . . Kenzie made me do it!"

"No, I didn't! It was your idea!"

"Was not!"

"Was!"

"Wasn't!"

"Was!"

"Wasn't!"

"Was!"

"Was!"

"Wasn't!"

"Ha!"

"Aubrey!" Kenzie complained. "Tell her that's not fair."

I sighed. "Both of you, go to your room!"

They did, sulkily. I rolled my eyes. "Nothing like sitting for twins."

"No kidding," Brooke agreed. "So, where is everybody?"

"Gone. I have four sitting charges, and three have been banned to bedrooms."

"Three?"

"Oh, right. Katie closed her sister in her room to stop her from pulling hair."

Brooke nodded. "Poor Cynthia. Having to deal with

that all day? I'd be bald, too, but that would be my own fault."

I giggled. "I'll say."

We sat and talked undisturbed until Mr. and Mrs. Hale came home. It was a productive job.

Chapter Nine:

Compared to Monday's job, the rest of the week was fairly uneventful. Before I knew it, we were gathered in my room on Friday, talking about how the fliers seemed to be working.

"Remember all those fliers we put in the grocery store?" Erin was saying. We nodded. "Well, I went there yesterday, and there were like, two left. I think we're about to save Cynthia's life."

"Again," Jenna added. Giggles erupted.

"No kidding," Brooke said. "You know, I haven't visited her since we all did, but I think she's pretty happy about it, right, Aubrey?"

"Yeah," I said. "And we have a lot in common. I think she and I are going to be best friends soon."

Everybody smiled. "That's great," Erin said. "You could always use another person to keep you from driving the rest of us up the wall," she joked. "Right, Jenna?"

Jenna jerked her head up. "Yeah. Sure."

I gave her a funny look. "Are you okay?"

"Yeah, I'm fine. Just thinking."

"About what?"

"Stuff. Like, what if we don't raise enough money?"

I frowned. "She's right. I've got baby toys, clothes I've outgrown, stuff I don't use, but that's all kids' stuff."

We all looked at the ground. "Yeah," Brooke said. "What if all those people show up and don't buy anything because it's not what they thought it'd be?"

"Let's just hope that doesn't happen," Erin said.

Still, my stomach flipped at the idea of us not being able to help Cynthia. She wouldn't get chemo, and she might . . . die! I felt sick all of a sudden. My legs were shaking. My heart was pounding. I felt like I was the one with cancer, the one who had to depend on everybody else, and I could only sit back and hope for the best. It was not a good feeling.

"Well," Brooke said. "We all have attics, so we could ask our parents to donate, too. That way we have things for adults and kids."

I nodded. "Yeah, that's a great idea!"

"And we're back to saving the day! Dun da-dun!" Jenna said.

"Okay, guys," Brooke said. "Settle down. We have to do this for Cynthia. It'll take a lot of planning and effort, so let's buckle down and plan, plan, plan."

"Alright," Erin said. "Well, we agreed to take inventory tomorrow, but we never decided where. Any suggestions?"

"There isn't enough room here," I pointed out.

"Ditto," Erin said.

"My house is a zoo on Saturdays," Jenna said, pretending to be a monkey.

We giggled.

"I guess that leaves my house," Brooke said. "Be there around four thirty . . . in the morning."

Jenna, who was on the bed with her, gave her a push. "That will never happen. Ever."

"In your dreams," I added.

Erin shook her head. "I don't care whether it's real or a dream; I will never get up at three a.m. in my life, so forget it altogether."

"Fine," Brooke said. "How about ten thirty a.m.?"

"Sure," I said.

"I'm free," Erin said.

"Let me check my schedule . . ."

"JENNA!" the three of us shouted.

"Ten thirty. Roger that."

Erin sat up on the floor. "I thought we were in the army, not in space, and if we are astronauts, I call Neil Armstrong. He-hem. 'That's one small step for man, one giant leap for mankind'."

We burst out laughing at her 'man' voice. She shrugged. "Just trying to play the part."

"Next time play the part of a millionaire that can just give Cynthia five hundred dollars," Brooke teased.

Erin stuck her tongue out.

"Alright," I said. "That's enough. Both of you, back to your corners. Cue gong."

That got us going again. Dad came in. "Sounds like the four of you are having a little too much fun in here."

We shook our heads, even though we probably looked like giggling bobble-headed idiots from where he stood.

When I saw his hand I stopped laughing. My friends followed. "Who 'ya holding on to?" I asked.

"Hi!" Melissa. *I should've guessed that,* I thought.

"Hi!" we replied.

"They're having a meeting," Dad explained.

"Oh," Jenna said. "That reminds me. I brought snacks. I've got M & Ms and Skittles."

"Right before dinner?" Melissa asked. "Your dad's making it."

"Gimme those!" I teased. Dad came in and pretended to whack me on the back of my head.

We passed out the snacks as my dad and Melissa went downstairs.

"Eep!" we said as soon as we were sure they were out of earshot.

"Does she live here now or something?" Brooke asked.

I shook my head. "She might as well, though."

"What do you mean?" Erin asked.

"Well, she comes almost every morning and as far as I know she stays through dinner."

"Do you think your dad will propose?" Jenna asked.

"Yeah." I really did, too.

"When?" Jenna prodded.

I shrugged.

"I hope soon. That way, they could have an outside wedding," Erin said.

"I dunno," I said. "I think my dad likes the idea of a small indoor gathering."

"Where?" Brooke asked.

"I think he'd like to have it in the garage."

My friends frowned. "Are you serious?" Jenna said.

I nodded. "Yeah. He told me that once when I was little. He said he'd want it to be near Christmas, and he'd decorate the garage so you wouldn't even know it was a garage."

"How?" That was Brooke.

"I think he'd put up garland and wreaths and candles, since our garage doesn't have much of a light."

"That would actually be romantic, if your guests could forget that they really are in a sweaty garage." Jenna made a face as she spoke.

I laughed. "Yeah. I just wonder what Melissa wants her wedding to be like."

I started imagining.

I imagined a hill near our house (not that there is a hill, but, hey, haven't I told you my imagination goes wild?). A big white arch stretched above the sunset. A pastor stood between my father and Melissa. On her side were me, Jenna, Brooke, and Erin. On Dad's side were Caleb, Logan, Tyler, and Seth. The flower girl was Grace Hale. The wind blew against Melissa's veil, and my hair swayed from side to side. The ceremony was about to end –

"See you tomorrow!" Erin called. I looked around. No one was there. Oops. I guess I would just have to wait for the next day.

Chapter Ten:

I woke up on Saturday with a jolt in my stomach, and surprisingly, I couldn't have felt better. I knew we could do it. We just had to work hard. I'd asked Dad about giving me some adult stuff to sell, and I had a pile of things. My dad had taken inventory the night before and typed up a list that looked like this:

- *fifteen shirts*
- *twenty pants*
- *ten skirts*
- *twelve pairs of shoes*
- *seven rattles*
- *eight clean teething rings*
- *three posters*
- *two lamps*

- *five rechargeable batteries*
- *twenty-seven Barbies*
- *nine baby dolls*
- *seven baby outfits*
- *one office set*
- *six board games*

I know. When I have something to do for charity I go all the way. That's a total of one hundred thirty-seven items (my dad told me). We pulled up in front of Brooke's house at 10:25. Five minutes to spare. I leapt out of my dad's car, grabbed the bags from his trunk, waved, and ran up to the front door.

"Hi!" I jumped a mile. Brooke was standing right behind me.

"Hi," I replied.

She looked at my bags. "That's a lot of stuff you got there. Come on. Everybody else is here. We're already pooling junk."

I giggled as we made our way into the garage. Everybody'd already started dumping stuff on the ground (just kidding). "Wow."

They nodded.

"You know," Erin said, trying to get to me through everything. "I know we weren't supposed to start organizing until tomorrow, but I'm thinking desperate times call for early organization."

We giggled, then nodded.

"So, how are we going to organize this stuff?" Jenna asked.

"Well," I suggested. "We could start by making two piles; kids, and adults."

So we did. We spent about an hour trying to sort everything out, but finally we had a kids' stack, and an adults' stack (and trust me, the kids' stack was a lot bigger.)

"Okay," Jenna said, "I'm not thinking that's gonna cut it."

Erin shook her head. "No, definitely not. Why don't we sort kids into older kids and babies?"

Well, that ate up another hour. At one o' clock, Brooke said, "You guys wanna go inside and eat lunch?"

We nodded, and followed her into the house. We were all dripping with sweat (sorry to gross you out, but it's almost the truth).

"Good afternoon, girls," Mr. McCully said. He was standing over the stove.

We shook our heads.

"More like hot afternoon," Jenna said.

"And stuffy garage," I added. We all started laughing. Mr. McCully looked at us as if we'd gone insane.

"Well," he said. "I'm making grilled cheese sandwiches for lunch. Sound appealing?"

"Uh-huh," I said.

"Sure," Erin replied.

"Yeah," Brooke said.

"Whatever, I don't care." That was Jenna.

He looked up. "You know, if we close the outside garage door, we can leave this door open, and that way you girls can have some air conditioning."

"OKAY!"

Brianna came into the room, looking like she just woke up. "I've started my beauty sleep."

We bit our lips to keep from laughing. It didn't work. "Well," Brooke remarked. "Looks like you might want to finish up."

"Ha ha, very funny."

"I thought so," I said. Jenna clamped her hand over my mouth.

We all giggled some more, then sat down at the kitchen table.

"Alright, gigglers, monsters, and gents. Lunch is served."

We ate, then got back to work. We got everything organized and ready to price, so we called off the next week's gatherings.

"So," Brooke said after we'd finished. "Who wants to have a slumber party over here tonight?"

"Me!" Jenna exclaimed.

"Sure," Erin said.

"Can't," I replied. "Melissa's coming over for dinner, and I promised her I'd be there. But we did get out of school yesterday, so we could have it tomorrow."

"Great," Brooke said.

"Good for me," Jenna replied.

"Yeah," Erin agreed.

"Okay," I said. "Where?"

"Zoo, remember?" That was, well, you probably know who it was (if you don't, it was Jenna).

I laughed. "We could have it at my house, but my room's kind of small."

"I have something called brothers," Erin said.

"Well, then," Brooke said. "We can have it here. We'll just go upstairs to my room and lock the door."

We giggled. Someone's car honked. It was Mrs. Morris.

"See you tomorrow, guys," Jenna said.

We waved.

Another car pulled in the driveway. It was my dad. I left.

In the car, Dad asked, "So, how'd it go?"

"We had over six hundred items," I reported. "Everybody had a list, so Erin calculated how much it was altogether."

"Ah."

The rest of the ride was silent.

That night, Melissa came to our house, we said hello, then I left her alone with my dad. The phone rang.

"Hello?"

"Hi, Aubrey. It's Jenna. How's the date going?"

"Fine. I mean, I haven't heard a thing."

"Do you think tonight might be the night?"

"No, probably not."

"Oh. Well, maybe next time."

I sighed. "Well, I haven't heard anything about it, so I'm hoping he wouldn't do it without telling me. Although, he might like for it to be a surprise."

"Would it be a pleasant surprise?"

"Sure. I like Melissa."

"But do you love her?"

"Huh?"

"Well, you're always talking about how she'll be your mother. Shouldn't you love your mother?"

"Well, yes. But she won't technically be my real mother."

"Do you love your father?"

"Of course I do. Why wouldn't I?"

"You would."

"So what's your point?"

"He isn't technically your *real* father. *He* lives in Japan."

I thought about that. She was right. "Well, he's raised me."

"He's only raised you this far. You still have a long way to go. I mean, through the rest of middle school, high school, and college. That's another eleven years. And what were you thinking when you first saw your dad?"

"I made a poopie?"

She laughed. "No. You didn't think anything. You were a helpless baby. Someone was taking care of you, and you had to trust them to put you in the right hands."

"What's your point?" I asked again.

"Well, you learned to love him, right?"

"Yeah."

"And he loved you when he first saw you, right?"

"Sure."

"Well, if he loves you so much, don't you think anyone he chose to be your mother would love you, too?"

"So you think Melissa loves me?"

"Well, think about it, Aubrey. If he asks her to marry him, what is she agreeing to?"

"Move in with us? Be Dad's wife?"

"No. She's agreeing to love not only your dad, but she's also agreeing to take you as her daughter. Isn't that true?"

I had to really think that one through. Finally, I said, "Yeah, that is true."

"So if she says yes, she must love your dad and you."

I smiled. "You're right."

"So do you love her?"

"I'm not sure. I have to think about it."

"Okay."

"See 'ya."

"'Bye."

I hung up, and spent the night really thinking about what Jenna had said. Did I love Melissa? Should I love Melissa? Should I be thinking this much about it? I had no clue.

Chapter Eleven:

"We're going . . . to Glendale . . . Uh-huh . . . Uh-huh . . . Oh, yeah . . . Bow chica wow-wow, chica wow-wow . . . Bow chica wow-wow, chica wow-wow . . . Bow chica wow-wow, chica wow-wow."

It was Saturday. A week had passed. I still hadn't decided whether or not I loved Melissa, but at the moment that was not my concern. We were on the way to the hospital again to see Cynthia. This time Mrs. McCully was off, so she was driving. We'd had soda before we left (can you tell?), and we were singing. I was surprised we hadn't been thrown out the window yet.

"Okay, girls, that's enough."

We were pulling into the parking lot. Our excitement boosted. We (well, most of us) hadn't seen Cynthia in awhile, and we were really psyched.

As soon as we brought our adult up to the information desk, the woman gave us the room number.

We rode the elevator silently (trying to make mind contact with the machine and tell it not to stop). When we got to the floor we wanted, we were led in while Mrs. McCully talked to Cynthia's parents.

"Hi, guys!" she said.

"Hi," we answered.

"How's everything going?"

"Pretty good," Brooke said. "I've checked everywhere we put your fliers, and they're all gone!"

"Really?"

We all nodded.

"Wow. I guess I underestimated you. When's the sale?"

"A week from today," Jenna reported. "We have a LOT of stuff to sell."

"Yeah," Erin said. "The McCullys will be happy when they can park in their own garage again."

Brooke sighed. "If only we used our powers for good."

"We do," I reminded her. "Hello. Person in a freaky hospital bed. We're saving her from-" My imagination got me again. This time, though, it was not good.

It was the twenty-fourth. We'd just closed the garage sale and were counting the money (okay, Erin was counting; the rest of us were pestering her to get it done). "Oh, no," Erin said.

"What?!"

"Well, minus the money needed to pay for the lemonade supplies, we made . . . this much." She handed us a piece of paper. We passed it around, gasping. It was .

. . a one dollar bill! We were $474 off our target! Cynthia couldn't get her chemo!

We were all crushed. It was our fault! We had said we'd do this and gotten her hopes up, and then we'd . . . we'd . . . we'd forgotten to put the signs up in the yard that said there was a sale!

The next day we went to the hospital to visit one more time. I walked bravely up to the bed Cynthia was still lying in. "We made one dollar for you."

"You did WHAT!?"

"We're really, really sorry!"

"SORRY!? What do you MEAN, you're SORRY!? I'm dead. My life is virtually OVER and all you have to say is SORRY?!"

Jenna shook her head. "We also wanted to say . . . lemonade?"

"NO! Get OUT!"

We were pulled into a black hole (I know), never to be seen again.

"Earth to Aubrey," Cynthia said.

"Augh!" I cried, jumping backwards.

Everyone looked at me. "What are you doing?" Erin asked.

"She's out to get us! Black hole! One dollar! Ooh!"

Cynthia put an angelic face on, then turned into a curious face. "Where do you go when you disappear?"

Jenna nudged her. "We've discovered that when she comes back like this, it's really best not to know."

I smirked at her, reality slowly coming back. "Sorry."

"You know, I'd love to hook a television screen to you," Cynthia said. "That way, whenever you left, we'd be able to see what you see. I don't know if you know this, but that would make our lives a whole lot easier."

I smiled at her. "Ha ha ha. I'm laughing, really. On the inside."

My friends laughed. "Sure you are," Brooke teased.

"Okay, my insides are shaking. That's their way of saying something's funny."

Four faces turned my way, slowly and cautiously. Then they turned away. "What are we going to do with you?" Erin asked.

"Me? You're the one who almost made us bury you in the backyard."

"Well," Cynthia said. "It's nice to know I'm not the only one in danger."

"Actually, it's her fault," Erin countered. "Remember?"

Cynthia gasped. "What'd I do?"

We explained the day of the fliers. Then, while we were laughing about it, a nurse came in and said it was time for us to go (Boo). Mrs. McCully came in, checked on Cynthia, then the five of us went out to the car.

That's when my friends burst.

"Is she coming tonight?" Jenna asked.

"Who?" I tortured her.

"MELISSA! Do you think tonight is the night?"

I sighed. "Sorry, they broke up."

"Awww." The three of them have amazing timing sometimes.

I burst out laughing.

"What's so funny?" Brooke asked.

"Gotcha!" I cried. "They're together. And she is

coming over tonight, just like every night. I'm not sure about a proposal, though."

My friends gently pushed me around. "That's not nice," Erin said, laughing.

Maybe not. But the truth was, I really wanted Dad to propose (even if I still wasn't sure if I loved her).

Chapter Twelve:

That night, Melissa showed up at six. Just like usual, we said hi, then I left. When I went upstairs, I called Jenna.

"Hello?" It was Faith.

"Hi, Faith. Can I talk to Jenna please?"

"May I ask who's calling?"

I rolled my eyes. "Faith, you know it's Aubrey."

"Yeah, but Daddy says always ask."

"Can you please just get your step sister?"

"Fine."

There was a long pause (big house). Finally, I heard Jenna. "She said yes, didn't she?"

"No. He hasn't asked yet. Listen, I've been thinking about what you said about loving Melissa."

"Yeah?"

"So, if I should love Melissa, do you love Tim?"

She sighed. "No, I don't. I really like him, but I have a real father out there."

"So do I," I countered.

"Yes, but yours lives in Asia. Your dad raised you and he's your dad. He has papers that say so."

"So? There are no papers out there that say if they get married Melissa will be my real mom, so why do I have to love her?"

"Because, your dad has never married, but he's still your dad. My mom was married, got divorced, and married again. If your dad marries, Melissa, in a way, won't be like Tim; she'll be like my dad, my mom's first marriage. Get it now?"

"But that makes no sense."

"Aubrey! That's what's wrong!"

"Thank you!"

"You're trying to find the sense in something that isn't sensible."

"Now I'm confused. You agree with me?"

"No, I don't. What I'm saying is, this is complicated, and there's no way to make it simple or for it to make sense. It just works out this way."

I thought about what she was saying. It was complicated, but it was starting to sink in.

"It seems to me that Melissa might not love you – at least at this point – as much as your dad does, because he was the one who raised you, but if she says yes, that means she loves you enough to call you her daughter. Now the question is, do you love her enough to call her your mother?"

That was tough. I wasn't sure. "I – I think so."

I could tell she was shrugging on the other end. "Well, you don't need to know, I guess. It was just something to think about. Well, if that's what you called about - "

"Ahhhhhhhh!!!"

"What was that?" Jenna asked.

"I don't know. I'll go see."

I walked downstairs. As soon as I turned the corner, I screamed, too. I couldn't believe what I was seeing.

Melissa was standing by her chair, but this was the unbelievable part: my dad was on one knee, holding out a ring.

"HE DID IT!" I screamed.

I went into Dad's office and picked up the phone.

"Did she say yes?"

"I don't know."

"W – W – W – Yes!"

"Okay. Now I do, and she did!"

After giving this some thought, she squealed. "I'm so happy for you! You are going to love having a mom!"

I smiled. "I am, aren't I?"

"Yeah. Listen, you go celebrate, and I promise I won't tell anyone."

"Thanks. I'll call you back later tonight, once I have the details."

"Okay. 'Bye."

"'Bye."

We hung up, and I raced into the dining room. Everyone was happy.

I just had one question. "Dad, why didn't you tell me?"

"Because I knew you'd like it, so I wanted to surprise both of you."

I hugged him. "Thanks."

He smiled. "Now. We don't have time to plan tonight, though."

We weren't listening. We were squealing. "I have a mom," I said.

"I have a daughter."

We didn't even notice the fact that Dad was giving us the strangest look in the world. It was a mix between his 'what-on-earth-are-you-doing' face and a face I vaguely remembered. "Wait," I said. "What's that face? The one besides the 'what-on-earth' face. I've seen it. Where?"

"So have I," Melissa said. "That's the face he just gave me right before you came downstairs."

He nodded. "And you know it because I looked at you like this when I first saw you."

"In Japan?" I asked.

"Yes, in Japan."

"Hoing ha!" Melissa and I said in unison.

We all laughed.

"Whoa," I said. "Does this mean we're moving?"

"No," Dad said. "Melissa will move in with us."

"Eeep," I said. "This is so exciting!"

"I know!"

My dad held his hands up. "Alright, alright. I know. Tomorrow, we can plan. Tonight, I want to call some people. Aubrey, you can use the house phone to call your friends, and if you want, I'll take you to Glendale tomorrow so you can tell Cynthia in person. How does that sound?"

"Good," I said.

"Great," Melissa replied.

I ran upstairs to make my phone calls. I started with Brooke.

"Hello?"

"Hi, Brooke. It's Aubrey, and she said yes!"

"No!"

"Yes!"

"Really?"

"Really!"

"Awesome!"

"I'm soooo excited!"

"You should be!"

"I couldn't wait to tell you guys!"

"Does Jenna know?"

"Yeah. I was on the phone with her when it happened."

She squealed. "Tell me everything you know."

"Unfortunately, I just did."

"Are you sure?"

"Positive!"

"Ooh, congratulations!"

"Thanks. Oh, and I almost forgot. I have to skip the pricing thing tomorrow."

"Wait, what? Why?"

"Oh, I'm still doing something that has to do with Cynthia."

"Like what?"

"Like going to see her. Dad's driving me."

"Oh, okay. Great! I think it's really great that you're spending all that time going to see her."

I smiled. "Yeah. I'll tell her the news then. I just had to call you guys, cause like I said, I couldn't wait to tell you!"

"Fantastic! Well, I'll let you keep calling people."

"Okay. 'Bye."

"'Bye."

We hung up, and I dialed Erin's number. Logan answered.

"Hi, Logan," I said. "Can I talk to Erin?"

"Sure."

A short pause followed. "Hi."

"She said yes!" I blurted out.

"Really?"

"Yes! But that's as far as the planning has gotten, but I'll tell you all about it as soon as I can!"

"Great! Thanks for calling, but Mom says it's time for dinner. 'Bye."

"'Bye."

I called Jenna and told her there was no plan. I went to bed that night happier than ever.

Chapter Thirteen:

"Good morning," I said to Dad when I went downstairs for breakfast the next morning.

He smiled. "It is a good morning."

I sat down. "So, when are we leaving?"

"As soon as you're ready."

I ate, got dressed, and went out to the car, followed by Dad. We drove to the hospital. I didn't even bother to ask the information desk for her room number; I had memorized it. I went up to the right floor, and found her parents, where they always sat, this time smiling.

I went into her room.

"Hi!" I said.

"Hey! This Saturday, right?"

I nodded. "Right."

"So, what brings you here? You were just here yesterday! I'm not that desperate for hope, am I?"

I giggled. "No. I'm here to tell you - "

"The garage sale isn't canceled, is it?"

I shook my head. "It's my dad."

"He broke up with Melissa?"

"NO! Just the opposite!"

"Are you serious?"

"No."

"Oh."

"YES I'm serious!"

She gave me a Look. "Not funny."

I nodded. "Yes, it was, actually."

We laughed.

"Alright, alright. Speaking of the garage sale - "

"We weren't."

"Weren't what?"

"Talking about the garage sale."

"Well, now that you bring it up, how's it going?"

I giggled. "Actually, it's going really well. They're over at Brooke's house pricing things."

"How many things do you have?"

"A lot."

"Wow. Thank you. Do you think you can do it?"

I nodded. "I know we can."

"Cheerleader."

"Rah! Rah!"

She laughed. "V-I-C-T-O-R-Y! What does that spell? Chemo!"

"Yeah. You keep believing that. Uh-huh."

"Eh. Spelling was never my best subject," she joked.

I giggled. "I can tell."

She nodded. "I'm a bad little girl."

"I know."

"Ugh!"

"Oh, my gosh! I'm just kidding!"

I looked out the window. A man with a baseball bat (and a security uniform) was chasing a woman with a spray can off the property, and she was trying to slow him down by spraying paint at him. I burst out laughing.

"What?"

"Oh, I wish you could see this."

"What's out there?"

I described the scene to her. She laughed.

"Wow. I've seen some pretty weird things out there, but nothing like that."

I nodded. "I've never seen anything like that."

A nurse came in, so I left.

As soon as we got home, we started planning.

"Where do you want the wedding to be?" Dad asked us.

I shrugged. "I don't care. Small or big is the first question."

"Small," they both said.

I wrote that down. "Well, if you wanted it to be in the garage, it would work."

"Okay, if we decorated it," Melissa said.

"When?" I asked.

"October," they both said.

"October . . ."

"Twenty-fifth," my dad answered.

"Okay. I think we've already covered all the basics except people," I said. "Maid of honor, Melissa?"

She smiled. "You."

"Why, thank you. Bridesmaids?"

"Jenna, Brooke, Erin, and Cynthia."

"Okay. Best man, Dad?"

"Tim."

"Got it. Groomsmen or ushers or whatever they're called?"

Dad smiled. "Caleb, Seth, Greg, and Tyler."

"Alright. On to little people. Ring bearer?"

"Logan."

I nodded. "Flower girl?"

"Flower girls," Melissa corrected me. "I know you think they're pains, but we've asked McKayla and McKenzie Hale to do it."

I sighed but wrote it down.

"I think we're done here if that's all we needed to know," I said, putting my paper away. "Thank you."

Dad nodded. "Anytime you'd like us to help with our wedding, just tell us," he joked.

I smiled, rolling my eyes.

"Oh," Melissa said. "We thought you would want to call and tell your friends so we didn't call them last night."

"Great," I said.

On my way up to my room, I thought. This wedding was definitely going to change my life – for the better.

Chapter Fourteen:

"No, no, no. That goes over there. Perfect."

It was Saturday. I was at Brooke's house, getting things organized. The sale was about to start and we were barely set up. Everything was literally going to be in the garage except the lemonade stand, so we had just closed the door so no one could get in early, but there was a line outside. We had everything in order except who was doing what.

We gathered in the far corner of the garage, near the door, where our counter was set up (it was hard to get in, so only the four of us had access to the house).

"Okay," I said. "I figure we need two people working the cash register, one person working the lemonade stand, and one person walking around. Who wants to take care of the walking?"

"I will," Jenna volunteered.

I nodded. "I figure we should let Brooke take care of the lemonade stand. Is that okay?"

"Sure," she said.

"So that leaves me and Erin to man the cash registers."

"There are two?" Erin asked.

I nodded again. "They aren't fancy. They just have money slots inside like cash registers do. We have two of them and two calculators."

We set up the registers, and Brooke walked through her house to the stand. We gave her a few minutes, figuring most people would be thirsty.

Then, at ten o' clock on the nose, I looked around. Everything was perfect, so I nodded to Erin. She pushed the button opening the garage. People stampeded in. I thought Jenna would get run over. She didn't though. She got the first official business of the day. People were calling her left and right. After about ten minutes, the crowd moved toward us. We were prepared.

For about two hours we had no break. At noon we closed for lunch and took inventory. Less than three hundred items remained.

We went inside. Mr. McCully was seated in the breakfast nook. We sat beside him.

"How's the selling going, girls?" he asked.

"Great," I said. "We've sold over half of everything."

He smiled. "What are you going to do with whatever you don't sell?"

Jenna shrugged. "Give it to charity."

"Well, good for you." We could all tell he was proud of us, and we were proud, too. We were just hot.

"I think you shouldn't worry about some other kid's

problem when you could keep the money," Brianna said.

Brooke smirked at her. "Whatever."

Erin was just kind of watching, as if she had no part in any of it. That was pretty smart of her, actually.

"We better get back out there," she said (it speaks!).

The afternoon was crazy, starting the second we got outside. Brooke ran up to us. "There's no more lemonade."

I ran inside and made more. Unfortunately, people were getting restless. Little kids who complained of thirst now were seeing toys they wanted.

I brought the lemonade carefully out to the stand. When I got back to where I was supposed to be there was a huge line on Erin's side. I took over my register, working like mad to make people happy.

"Who knew what we were getting ourselves into?" Erin said during a lull.

"I know," I replied. "It's driving me insane!"

She giggled. People were starting to line back up, though, so we couldn't talk anymore.

The peace only lasted about an hour. So many people started coming in that even with two lines there were people outside waiting to pay. We finally had to strip Jenna from her job and put her up with another register (luckily we found a register and a calculator). That settled people down a little.

But still, the quiet wasn't worth betting on. The next problem ended up being that we were completely out of lemonade, inside and outside.

When it happened, Brooke raced up to us. "We're out of lemonade."

I shrugged. "I'll just go make more."

She shook her head. "I've tried. We're all out."

I went into panic mode. I looked at my watch and relaxed. "It's already three. We close for the day in one hour, so you can just take Jenna's old job."

Jenna backed up. "No way. She can have this one. I'll take settling fights old ladies have over this."

So they switched.

Luckily that was the last problem for the day, because, man, solving them was getting old.

At exactly four o' clock we shut the garage door, then practically fell down with fatigue.

"How many years have we been out here?" I asked.

"Three and a half hours since lunch," Brooke answered. I knew she was right, but that doesn't mean I believed it.

We leaned on the table. "Who wants to count money and who wants an extra trip to the hospital?" Jenna asked. "'Cause I can't do either."

"I'll count," Erin said.

"I'll double-count what she counted," Brooke offered.

"I'll go tell Cynthia the news."

I almost fell asleep.

"Just not now," I added. No one laughed. It wasn't supposed to be funny.

At any rate, we got our energy back and the girls started counting the money.

"Whoa," Erin said after she counted.

"Whoa," Brooke said after her turn.

"What?" Jenna and I said in unison.

Erin caught her breath. "We have . . ."

"Enough?" I asked.

"Oh, yeah," Brooke answered.

"We made," Erin started again, "only . . . $679.43!"

We shrieked. That was $200 more than we needed!

"Hey, guys," I said.

"What?"

"What would you think about letting Cynthia join the club?"

"It'd definitely help next time we did this," Jenna joked.

"It's a great idea!" Erin said.

"I love it!" Brooke exclaimed.

I couldn't wait for the next day, the day I went to the hospital.

Chapter Fifteen:

"Go on up," the lady at the information desk told Dad and me. We were once again at the hospital.

We took the elevator up to Cynthia's floor. Her parents were waiting for us nervously. While Dad went to talk to them, I went into Cynthia's room.

"Hi." She didn't seem too happy.

"How are you?"

"Nervous. This is basically life or death for me. How are you?"

"Happy."

"Why?"

I shrugged. "I don't know."

"I'm gonna die."

I gave her a stern look. "Now you promised not to say that again until you knew the number. Do you want this check?"

She nodded.

"All right. Well, first of all, I want to tell you about your garage sale."

"Please, Aubrey. Just tell me. How much did you make?"

"I'm not going to. But I will tell you one thing."

"What?"

"Well . . . you're getting chemo!"

"You're kidding!"

I shook my head. "Nope."

"Well, how much? Come on. Please?"

"First let's talk."

"About what?"

"What do you mean, about what?"

"Well, I already know what's happening in your life, and I'm pretty sure vice versa."

"No. How did the twins react when they found out they were going to be in my dad's wedding?"

She laughed. "Well, first they stomped around the house saying they were too old to be flower girls, but when Mom told them they didn't have to wear their bracelets to the wedding, they started dancing around singing – well, chanting – 'in your face'."

I laughed, too. "Hey, Cynthia," I said.

"Hmm?" I could tell she was trying to X-ray vision the envelope.

"Why do your brothers and sisters think you aren't bald?"

She sighed. "Because Mom makes me wear a wig when I'm at home so I don't freak Grace out. I told her to throw it away this time when I met you guys, so she did."

"What about here?"

"Here they aren't allowed to see me."

I nodded. "Oh."

"Now can I *please* have that check?"

"Fine."

I handed it to her. She ripped the envelope open, took the check out, and dropped it. "I think I need glasses. Did that say you raised almost seven hundred dollars?"

"Yup."

"But that's two hundred more than we needed."

"Well, we figured your family could probably always use a financial boost."

She nodded. "We could. We had to dip into our emergency savings to pull out forty-five hundred."

"By how much?"

"Two hundred dollars. You saved me again. You're angels."

I smiled. "Do you want to join us?"

"Really?"

"Once you get out of the hospital."

She nodded again. "Thanks. You saved my life . . . literally."